Sandy Seal

HAPPY READING!

This book is especially for:

_____

Suzanne Tate
Author—
brings fun and
facts to us in her
Nature Series.

James Melvin
Illustrator—
brings joyous life
to Suzanne Tate's
characters.

Author Suzanne Tate
and
Illustrator James Melvin

Sandy Seal

A Tale of Sea Dogs

Suzanne Tate

Illustrated by James Melvin

Nags Head Art

To Nellie Myrtle

who loved the seashore
and all its natural treasures

Library of Congress Control Number 2004110339
ISBN 978-1-878405-49-4
ISBN 1-878405-49-7
Published by
Nags Head Art, Inc., P.O. Box 2149, Manteo, NC 27954
Copyright © 2004 by Nags Head Art, Inc.

Sandy Seal was a seal pup.
Her head looked like a dog
with no ears!

But Sandy was much different from a dog.
She had flippers and lived
in the sea.

Sandy Seal could swim and dive in just
a few hours after she was born!

But she was a mammal and couldn't live
without her mother's milk.

Sandy's mother often nursed her
while lying on the beach.
Other seal mothers were there too,
giving milk to their pups.

The big sea dogs lay on their sides.
They looked like giant bananas!

HUMANS walked along the beach one day.
The shy mother seals were scared
and slipped quickly into the sea!

"Maaa, Maaa!" Sandy cried. "Wait for me!"
But her mother didn't come back to get her
until the HUMANS went away.

One day, Sandy was diving with her mother.
The big seal was catching fish to eat.

Suddenly, a hungry tiger shark
swam near them!

"Help, Maaa!" Sandy cried. "I'm scared!"
"Quick!" her mother said. "Climb up on my back."

Sandy held on tightly with her front flippers.
Mother and seal pup swam quickly
away from danger!

"That was scary!" Sandy sighed.
Her big dark eyes looked bigger than ever.
"Just stay near me," her mother said,
 "and you will be safe."

But in only four weeks after birth, Sandy was
old enough to be on her own!
She had gained a thick layer of blubber
from her mother's rich milk.

Sandy's mother knew that it was time
to say goodbye.
She swam away fast!

"Where are you going?" cried Sandy.
Her big eyes looked sad.

But it was Mother Nature's way!
She had to take care of herself
from that day on.

Sandy dived everyday for food
— shrimp or small fish.
She stayed alone most of the time.

Sometimes, she would rest in the water
with other young seals.
All of them rested with their heads up
— looking like floating bottles!

Sandy Seal grew larger and swam south
to warmer waters.
Other animals were there too — porpoises
and young humpback whales.

Sandy watched the whales catch food
with their big wide mouths.

"I know the whales won't hurt me," Sandy thought.
"They only want little fish to eat."

When she was tired, Sandy pulled herself
onto the beach.
She growled —

Grrrrrr!

— if other seals came too near.

One day, Sandy had a fever and felt bad.
"I'll rest on that sandy beach," she thought.

The young sea dog swam close to the shore.

Sandy slowly pulled herself
out of the water.

HUMANS came along and saw her
lying on the sand.

"Oh, let's help the young seal. Look at its sad eyes,"
one of them said. "I think that it's cold.
Here's a blanket we can put over it."

"Wait! Seals don't need blankets," a little girl said. "We shouldn't touch it! Let's tell the people who care for sick seals."

HELPFUL HUMANS came to get Sandy.
They were careful to watch out
for her sharp teeth!

HELPFUL HUMANS put Sandy in a dog crate.
They took her to a special place for sick seals
and gave her food and medicine.

Sandy began to feel much better!

Soon, Sandy Seal was well enough to go home.
HELPFUL HUMANS took her to the beach.

They watched as the young sea dog pulled
herself into the sea.

"I'm a seal of approval for HELPFUL HUMANS,"
Sandy thought.
Then, she flipped her flippers
and swam away in the sea.